Chieko and the Pine
A Japanese Folktale

W9-DFF-043

By Steven Gregory

Illustrated by Takashi Ijichi

Text copyright © 2009 by Steven Gregory
Illustrations copyright © 2009 by Takashi Ijichi

All rights reserved. No part of this book may be reproduced or used in any form or by any means, electronic or mechanical, including photocopying, recording, or any information storage and retrieval system, without written permission from the publisher.

Tales Alive! Publishing, 6221 Lake Apopka Place, San Diego, CA 92119

www.talesalive.com

ISBN 13: 978-0-9800880-2-1

Library of Congress Control Number: 2008908056
p. cm.

Summary: One night while playing the koto in a remote mountain village, Chieko hears a mysterious flute player. For many nights Chieko and Matsuo play together, but when a mighty pine tree is needed for the village bridge, Matsuo disappears. After finding his flute where the tree was felled, Chieko plays her koto by the bridge where their music is heard again through the village.

The illustrations in this book were done using Japanese sumi-e ink and gansai
on rice paper with Japanese sumi-e brush.

Printed in China

10 9 8 7 6 5 4 3 2 1

First Edition, 2009

To my parents, Tom and Gloria,
who gave me a love of story.
- S.G.

To all my students,
who continue to inspire me.
- T.I.

Long ago in Japan, at the base of a great mountain, there stood a mighty pine tree. The tree was older and taller than all around it, yet its branches were as green and strong as any other. On the other side of the mountain was a small village that was surrounded by trees.

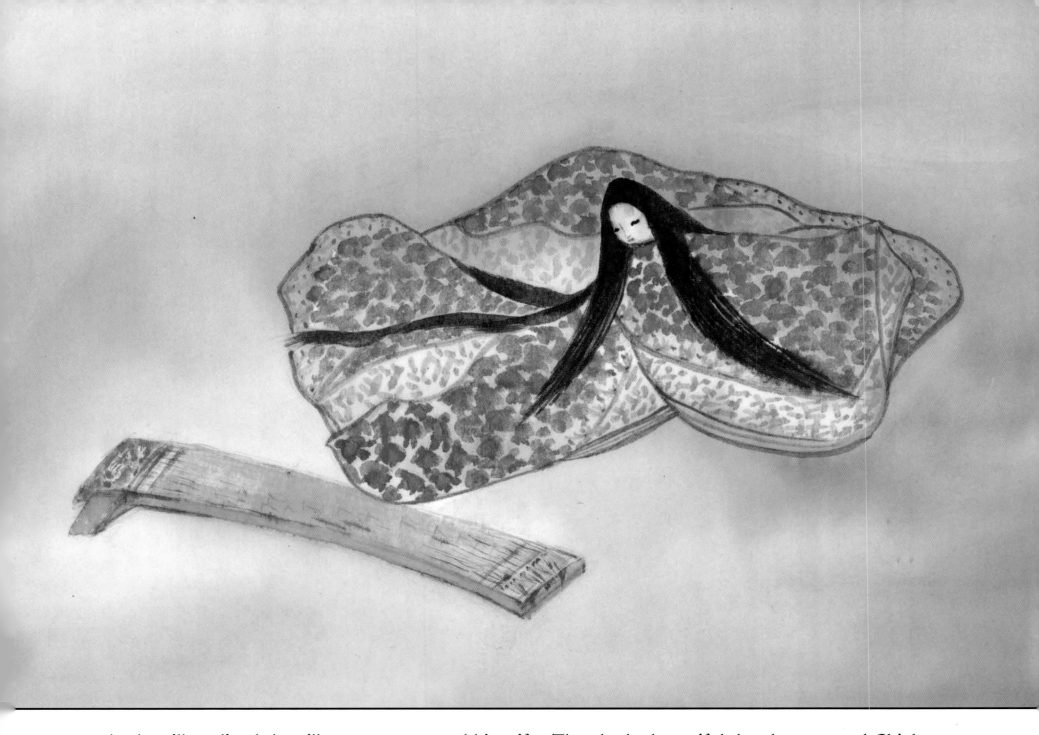

In the village lived the village governor and his wife. They had a beautiful daughter named Chieko, "child of a thousand branches." Chieko played the koto and would often play in the evening, the sounds drifting out into the forest.

One night as Chieko was playing the koto, she heard the sound of a flute accompanying her coming from the forest. For hours the two played together, their beautiful music rising and falling in perfect harmony.

When Chieko finished, she was filled with excitement. She waited for the mysterious flute player to come out of the forest and into the moonlight, but no one came.

The following night, Chieko played her koto again. The music drifted out into the forest. Soon, she heard the sound of the flute accompanying her once more. Chieko stopped.

"Please," she said, "show me who you are."

A young man stepped from the forest. He was handsome, tall, and wore a green kimono. In his hands he carried a flute.

He walked to the deck and stood only a few feet from where Chieko sat with her koto.

"Who are you?" Chieko asked.

"My name is Matsuo," the young man said. "I live on the other side of the mountain. I have listened to you for many nights, and only last night did I find the courage to play with you."

Matsuo kneeled down and began to play his flute. Chieko plucked the strings of her koto. Their music filled the forest for hours.

Matsuo stood up. "I must leave now," he said.

"Will I see you again?" Chieko asked.

"Yes," the young man said, then turned and walked into the forest.

Matsuo returned the next night and for many nights after that.

One day in the spring, Chieko's father received a message — the bridge that the people of the village used had been destroyed by a recent storm. Chieko's father told the villagers to search the forest for a tree from which to build a new bridge.

That night, the young man came to play once more with Chieko. But this time he seemed sad and troubled. As he rose to leave, he told Chieko he would not be able to return. Matsuo walked into the dark forest. Chieko ran after him.

But when she reached the forest, he was nowhere to be seen. Chieko heard the sound of Matsuo's flute fading off in the distance.

The next day, two messengers came to Chieko's father. A great pine tree had been found on the other side of the mountain. It would make a perfect bridge. Chieko's father was pleased and told them to gather some people to cut it down at once.

One of the messengers returned to Chieko's father the following day.

"We have chopped down the tree," he said, "but it is so large that we cannot move it to the river. We need help."

Chieko's father ordered all the people of the village to go with him to the other side of the mountain. Chieko went also.

When the villagers arrived, they were amazed at the size of the pine tree. The branches had been cut away, but the log was so heavy that it lay on the ground where it had fallen.

Ropes had been tied to it and the people pushed and pulled, but the tree could not be moved.

Chieko stared at the tree. There was something about it that seemed familiar to her. She walked over and looked carefully at it. She laid a hand on the tree and it shivered.

"Look!" the people said. "It moves!"

Inside her heart Chieko heard the sound of a flute and knew.

"I am here, Matsuo," she said. "I am here."

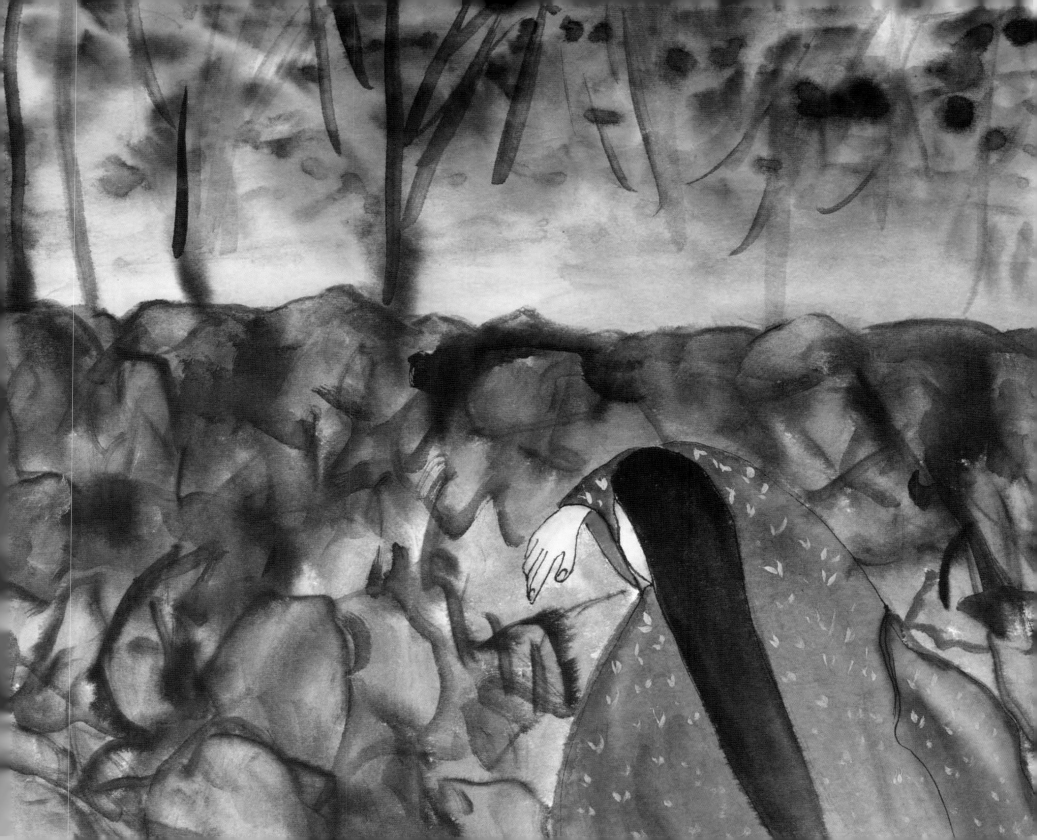

The tree seemed to move on its own.

"Pull!" the people shouted. "Pull it to the river!"

With her hands on the tree, Chieko led the people down to the river with the great pine.

In the river, the tree began to float. The people cheered as they floated the log down the river.

Chieko walked back to where the tree had fallen. There, on the ground, she saw Matsuo's flute. Reaching down, Chieko picked it up and held it close to her heart. She took the flute home and kept it with her always.

A new bridge was built that stood for generations over the river by the village.

Some evenings, Chieko would go down to the river and play her koto on the new bridge. On those nights, the sound of Matsuo's flute could be heard playing with her, their beautiful music drifting through the trees that surrounded the village.